Julia's Words

Judith L. Roth

Illustrated by

Brooke Rothshank

Herald Press

Scottdale, Pennsylvania
Waterloo, Ontario

Library of Congress Cataloging-in-Publication Data
Roth, Judith L.
  Julia's words / by Judith L. Roth ; illustrated by Brooke Rothshank.
      p. cm.
   Summary: While camping, a girl learns to experience the world more fully through all of her
senses as her new deaf friend, Julia, teaches her to communicate through sign language.
   ISBN 978-0-8361-9417-3 (pbk. : alk. paper)
   [1. Deaf–Fiction. 2. Camps–Fiction. 3. American Sign Language–Fiction. 4. Friendship–Fiction.
  5. Senses and sensation–Fiction. 6. People with disabilities–Fiction.] I. Rothshank, Brooke, ill. II. Title.
   PZ7.R72787Jul 2008
   [E]–dc22
                                             2008013315

To order or request information please call
1-800-245-7894 or visit www.heraldpress.com.

Most important of all,
continue to show deep love for each other,
for love makes up for many of your faults. . . .
God has given each of you some special abilities;
be sure to use them to help each other,
passing on to others God's many kinds of blessings.
— 1 Peter 4:8, 10 (*The Living Bible*)

For Georgie

and for Clayton and Kathy,
for welcoming me into their world. —JLR

When I first met Julia
she couldn't talk to me
because her hands were full.
So she set the buckets down. . . .

Later I set the words down
in my camping trip journal.

<u>June 17—Monday</u>
Julia talks with her hands.
I met her today at the campground beach.
She was shaping castle towers
and then she started
shaping words in the air.
I couldn't understand most of it,
but Julia handed me a shovel
and showed me where to dig.
You don't need many words
to build a sand castle together.

When it started raining,
Julia waved and we ran to her tent.
The rain pounded so loudly on the walls,
I covered my ears, wondering
why Julia looked at me strangely.
Then I figured it out—
Julia couldn't hear the rain.

June 18—Tuesday
Julia tugged me out of my sleeping bag
this morning.
She had seen Mom and Dad's bike.

It's hard to ride a bicycle built for two
with someone who can't hear.
You can't look at each other's faces.
You can't shout instructions.
You are balancing on two thin tires
and one long clumsy frame.
It's painful.
Julia taught me the word for blood—
touching the red of her lips
and dribbling her fingers down the back of her
hand.
This is a sign I will never forget.
I'll have the scars to remind me.

Later
I'm starting to think this might be too hard.
How can you be friends with someone
when you never really know
what that person is thinking?

By a trail we saw while biking,
we found a gravestone carved,

Joshua Trenton
1912-1914
With the Angels

I know Julia was sad by the look on her face.
But I wanted to talk about the baby who'd died,
not just be sad.
Then Julia closed her eyes and felt each letter.
I did it too.
It was like my heart heard a whole different story.

<u>June 19—Wednesday</u>
Julia led me to the stables today
and we went horseback riding.
I noticed how much it fills up your senses.
There's the smell of horse and leather.
You see the world from higher up.
You sway, your whole body does.
You hear the clop of hooves
and the squeak of the saddle
and blowing from the horse's nose and mouth.

Except you don't hear that if you're Julia.
I wanted to cover my ears to find out how Julia felt,
but my hands were full of reins.
I closed my eyes instead.
The reins in my hands were soft and thick.

We went on a night hike tonight
with the ranger and our flashlights
and a whole bunch of strangers.
In a clearing in the forest
we stood circled, holding hands,
flashlights off and stuffed into pockets.
The ranger wanted us to hear an owl call.
There was no moon.

Julia squeezed my hand.
I think she was wondering what we waited for.
But I didn't know the sign for owl.
And she couldn't have seen it anyway, it was so dark.
I shook my head close to her face
so she could feel my no-answer.
She squeezed my hand harder.

I would like to ask Julia this one thing:
If you know the world only by seeing and touching,
how bad does it feel when the lights go out?
But I don't know how to ask her.

<u>June 20 — Thursday</u>
Julia wasn't in my tent this morning when I woke up.
I thought, Fine, I'll go meet that girl I saw in the trailer.
So I did.
The new girl could hear and talk.
But her words didn't match her face.
It made me wonder if you ever really know
what someone else is saying.

I went to find Julia.
She wasn't at her campsite.
And she wasn't in the bathrooms.
And she wasn't fetching water from the tap.
For a minute I thought, *What if I never see her again?*

It was close to our seashell-hunting time,
so I went down to the beach.
Every other day, Julia has raised her hands
over her head like a champion
when she found the best shell.
She's a good finder.
Today I found a sand dollar—whole.
It fit the palm of my hand like a fancy cookie.
I almost crushed it when I saw Julia hunting
without even a smile for me.

She looked mad and I remembered
how she'd squeezed my hand last night.
I went close to her
and made my face into a question.

She threw a rock into the water,
picked up a stick and wrote in the sand,
"You give up too easy.
Find a way to tell me."
I picked up another stick,
but she knocked it from my hand.

She wanted me to tell her
like I should have in the dark.
It was hard to think, but
I held her hand like last night,
and moved our hands in beats
and touched her ear.

Julia smiled.
"Waiting to hear what?" she wrote
and handed me her stick.
"Owl."
Julia showed me the signs
for *owl* and *waiting* and
asked if I'd heard the owl.
When I shook my head No,
she signed, *Me too.*
Then she saw my shell
and raised my champion arms for me.

<u>June 21—Friday</u>
Today we did last-time things.
Last-time shell hunt.
Last-time castle.
Last-time breaking our bones on the tandem.
When we'd finished,
Julia's family came over
for a farewell weenie roast.

After S'mores, we bundled up in blankets
while our parents told spooky stories.
Julia's mom and dad signed them for her.
I dozed off watching the shadows of their hands flickering.
Julia's words are like chocolates
you can taste with your eyes.
Or songs you can hear without ears.
One day, I will have all the words I need
to tell Julia anything.

Words Julia Taught Me

Water

Bicycle

Blood

Owl

Cat

Horse

<u>June 22—Saturday</u>
Julia's gone.
She taught me one last sign this morning—*forever*.
The curving motion fit my hand
like a dance I already knew.
And just before her family drove away,
we signed *friends forever*
to each other through the car window.
It felt like our words began a long road
we would go down together.

Friends forever, Julia and I.

Waiting

Stars

Chocolate

Together

Friends

Forever

Dear Christina,

My parents say you can visit the whole last week of July. Want to come?

Love, Julia

The Author

Judith L. Roth has been an editor and a youth minister. Her poetry has appeared in more than a dozen magazines. She is a songwriter and writes biblical study books, but her first love is children's fiction. Besides writing, she works as an interpreter of American Sign Language for students with hearing impairments. She holds a master's in theology from Fuller Theological Seminary. Her book *Cups Held Out* was published in 2006.

The Illustrator

Brooke Rothshank is a painter and illustrator who has an affinity for working in glass, portraiture, and art for children. Her works have been exhibited at the Chicago International Miniature Exhibit and the Andy Warhol Museum. She holds a bachelor's in painting from Goshen (Indiana) College. Brooke illustrated *Cups Held Out*, published in 2006.